Designed by Flowerpot Press
in Franklin, TN.
www.FlowerpotPress.com
Designer: Stephanie Meyers
Editor: Johannah Gilman Paiva
DJS-0912-0137
ISBN: 978-1-4867-0856-7
Made in China/Fabriqué en Chine

Prospero-
A powerful wizard and former Duke of Milan.

Good trait:
A loving father. Being very clever, he loves books.

Not so good trait:
Quite stubborn. Neglectful of his duties.

Prospero

Miranda-
Prospero's daughter.

Good trait:
Strong. Kind. Compassionate.

Not so good trait:
Being the heroine of the story, she has none.

Miranda

Setting:
A deserted island, with hints of magic, in the Mediterranean Sea, near Italy.

Ariel-
A powerful spirit and Prospero's servant. How he became a servant, we will soon find out . . .

Good trait:
Powerful. Helpful.

Not so good trait:
He doesn't really have any bad traits—he just wants to be released to go home.

Ariel

Alonso-
The King of Naples.

Good trait:
Quick to admit when he has done wrong.

Not So good trait:
Easily influenced by others (and I'm sure we can all agree that a good king must lead and not follow).

Alonso

The **Captain** and his **crew**, who are asleep for most of the story, for reasons we will soon discover...

Antonio-
Prospero's brother
and currently the
Duke of Milan. Aha!
The plot thickens.

Good trait:
Hardworking.

Not so good trait:
Seeks power, even
if he has to steal it.

Antonio

And so our
story begins...

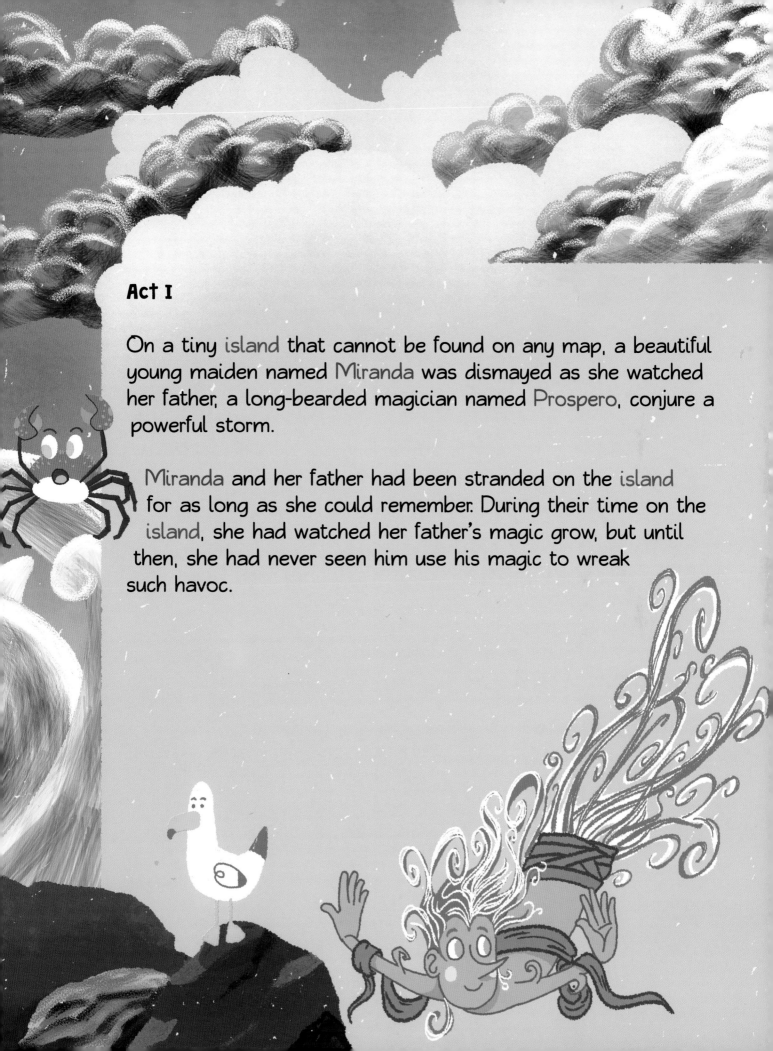

Act I

On a tiny island that cannot be found on any map, a beautiful young maiden named Miranda was dismayed as she watched her father, a long-bearded magician named Prospero, conjure a powerful storm.

Miranda and her father had been stranded on the island for as long as she could remember. During their time on the island, she had watched her father's magic grow, but until then, she had never seen him use his magic to wreak such havoc.

"Oh please, Father!" Miranda cried, "Why have you created this storm? What about those poor sailors?" The powerful Prospero circled his magic staff round and round, creating fierce gusts of wind.

"Don't worry, dear!" he called over his shoulder to his daughter. "I have a plan. They will not be injured—my servant Ariel is watching over them as we speak."

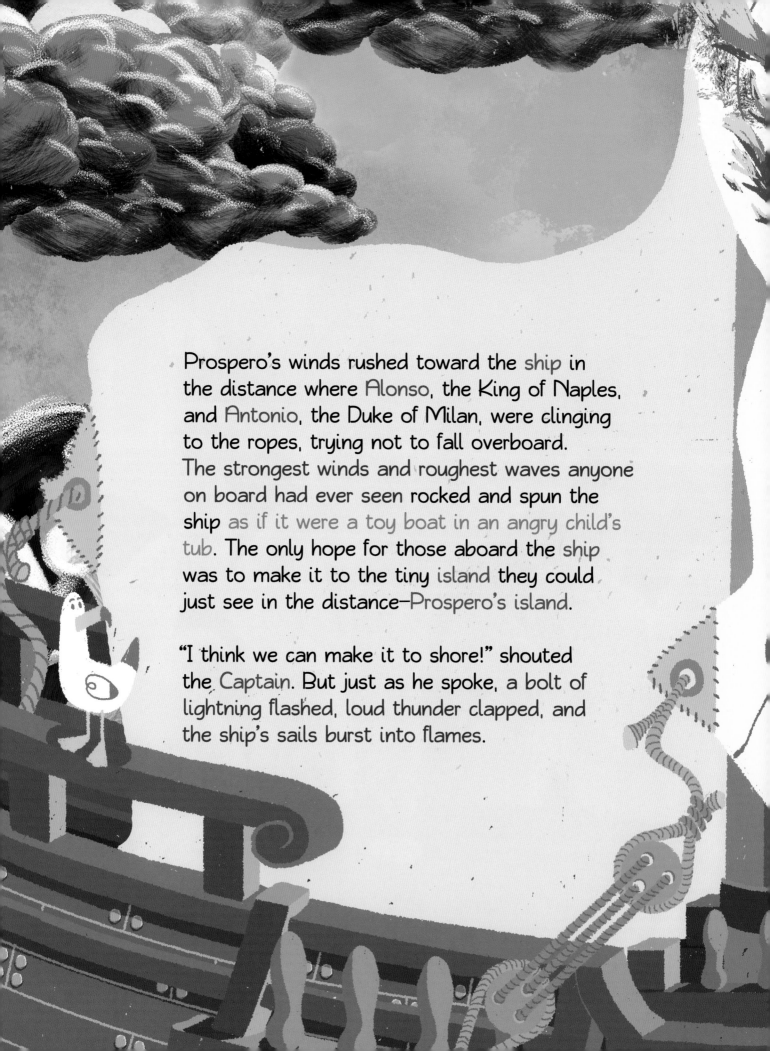

Prospero's winds rushed toward the ship in the distance where Alonso, the King of Naples, and Antonio, the Duke of Milan, were clinging to the ropes, trying not to fall overboard. The strongest winds and roughest waves anyone on board had ever seen rocked and spun the ship as if it were a toy boat in an angry child's tub. The only hope for those aboard the ship was to make it to the tiny island they could just see in the distance—Prospero's island.

"I think we can make it to shore!" shouted the Captain. But just as he spoke, a bolt of lightning flashed, loud thunder clapped, and the ship's sails burst into flames.

"Abandon ship!!!" called the Captain. Antonio and the King leapt from the ship and paddled with all of their might through the waves, toward the island.

Now, had Antonio or the King looked back, they might have noticed after they jumped, the flames began to die down, the seas began to calm, and a glimmer was in the air above the ship where the now-fast-asleep Captain and his crew lay. You see, Ariel had cast a spell of deep sleep and protection over them. But the two nobles never looked back—they just kept swimming.

As the King and Antonio made it to shore, exhausted and as wet as puddles, they collapsed on the beach and promptly fell into a magical sleep. Prospero was pleased as he watched them through his spyglass. For twelve years he had been stranded on this island waiting for this day, practicing his magic all the while.

It was on the very beach where the King and the Duke now slept that Prospero had found the spirit Ariel, who had been trapped by unknown magic long ago in an old, gnarled tree. Prospero had freed Ariel from the tree—only to make him a servant, in anticipation of this very day.

You see, in his old life, Prospero had been the Duke of Milan. He and his daughter, Miranda, lived in an enormous castle filled with suits of armor, beautiful fountains, lush gardens, and Prospero's favorite thing in all the world—books. Prospero had particularly come to love magic books. In fact, he seemed to do nothing else but study them. He left all of the official Duke work to his brother, Antonio, who seemed to enjoy the meetings, maps, tax accounts—and power—a great deal more than he did.

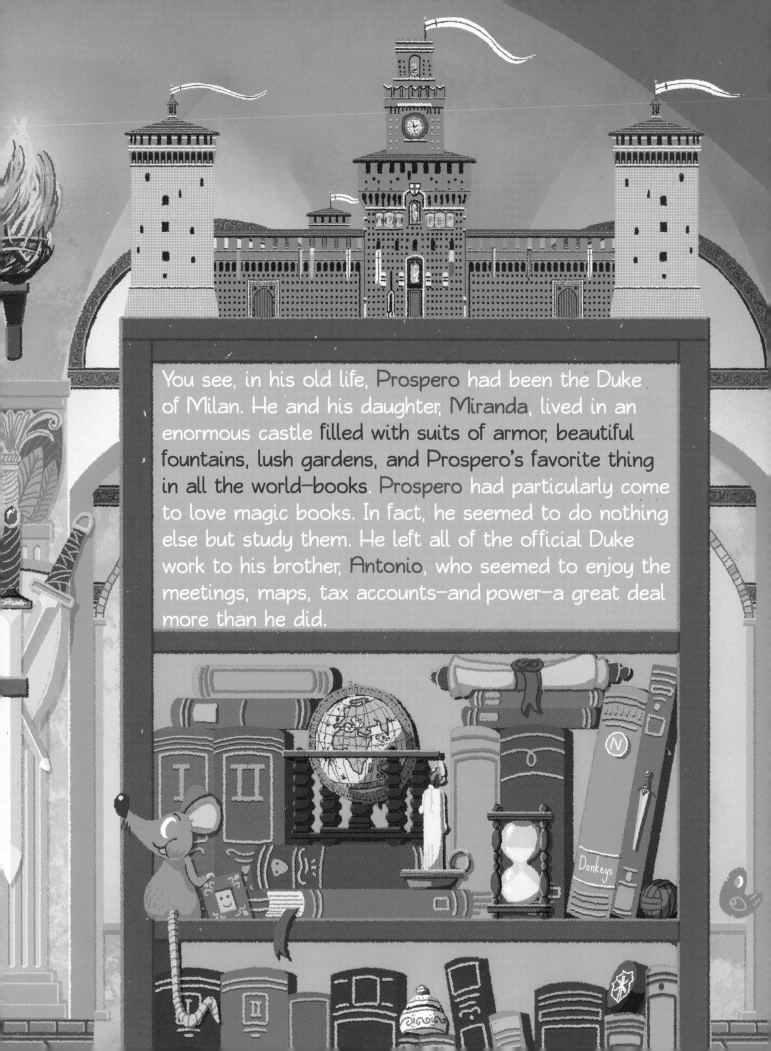

Anger and jealousy began to grow in Antonio's heart as he realized he was doing all of the work. He decided HE should be the Duke of Milan. Antonio secretly met with the King, who unfortunately agreed. So they put Prospero and Miranda in a boat just big enough for two, and sent them off to sea in the middle of a storm. That is how Prospero and Miranda ended up on this tiny island in the Mediterranean Sea.

Act II

King Alonso and Antonio were fast asleep on
the beach, but as Ariel's magic began to recede,
Antonio rose from his slumber. He was groggy
from the magic, and cross that he was now
stranded on this island because of a treacherous
boat ride the King had made him embark upon.
(Kind of ironic don't you think?) Antonio looked
at the still-slumbering King, and villainous thoughts
began to bubble and boil in his brain. What if the King were never to
wake? Perhaps if King Alonso's brother were in charge instead, there
would be no more excursions across the sea . . .

As Ariel finished removing his charms, and the King slipped his bonds
of sleep, Antonio's fantasies fled his mind as quickly as they had
entered. Perhaps it was just the sun and the near-drowning getting
to him. Perhaps it was just his ferocious hunger affecting his thinking.
Either way, he shouldn't be thinking such thoughts.

Act III

Antonio wasn't alone in his ravenous desires, though. When King Alonso awoke, he too, was starving. It was as if their hunger had magically materialized a hundred times stronger than a moment before. And the smells! Where were those magnificent smells coming from?

How disappointed these two would be if they knew there was no feast at the end of those smells, but only the meddling of magic. You see, Prospero had instructed Ariel to lead the King and his brother around the island, chasing after whiffs of the most delectable delights. The smells were nothing more than another testament to the powerful magic of Ariel and plotting of Prospero.

Miranda looked through her father's spyglass and frowned. "Father, why would you do that to those poor men?"

Prospero told her that they were the very men who had put them on this island, and he had been waiting for this day for a dozen years.

Miranda shook her head, unsure what to think.

"Do not fear for these shipwrecked men," said Prospero. "They are unharmed, and shall remain so. Why, even their clothes are as fresh as the day they first set sail. Now, my dear, leave me in peace while I decide how this day shall end."

Miranda had never seen this side of her father before. She was shocked at the story of her uncle's betrayal, but frightened by her father's powerful magic as well. She trusted him, but she did have one question for him before she left, "Father, why have we been on this island for so long when your magic seems to be powerful enough to have built us a ship and sailed us home?"

That was an excellent question indeed, and one Prospero hadn't actually thought of before.

Act IV

Prospero sat down on a rock and contemplated the last twelve years. It had been wrong what his brother had done to him. Antonio had all but sentenced Miranda and Prospero to death when he put them in that boat. However, Prospero loved his daughter more than he wanted revenge on his brother.

For Miranda's sake, Prospero could forgive Antonio.
She would never have a normal life here on this island.

It was time for Ariel to bring King Alonso and Antonio
back to Prospero's beach. Prospero called
for Ariel and ordered him to bring the
shipwrecked crew to him at once.

Act V

Ariel flitted across the island, and returned with the exhausted, starving, and disappointed Antonio and King Alonso trailing behind him. Though Prospero was still angry with his brother for what he had done, as he saw these miserable men trudging towards them, all he could think was that it was time to reconcile.

As Ariel presented the shipwrecked men before his master, Prospero's heart began to change. He was ready to put an end to this day and the past twelve years. He was ready to give Miranda a new future. It was time to return to Milan.

First, it was time to reveal the truth to the stranded nobles.

"Gentlemen," announced Prospero. "I am the magician who has brought you to this island."

The two men crouched in fear as Prospero stood and raised his magic staff over his head.

"I have made magic too important for too long, and I am sorry," declared Prospero as he shattered the staff over his knee.

With the source of Prospero's magic gone, the skies cleared,
and the two men immediately recognized Prospero.

"Brother!" cried Antonio with fear in his voice.

Prospero approached Antonio and embraced him. "What you did
to me was wrong, brother, but I want to forgive you."

Antonio wasn't sure exactly what was happening, but he was
happy his brother hadn't used his staff on him.

Next, Prospero happily approached King Alonso.

"Have no fear," he told the King. "Your ship and all the people aboard are well."

Prospero called for Ariel and asked him for one last service: to wake the crew, and bring the mended ship to shore so everyone could sail home.

Prospero set Ariel free from his servitude and apologized for saving him from a tree only to make him work for all these years. Ariel forgave Prospero and promptly disappeared with a pop.

At first, Prospero's anger began to boil back up when King Alonso asked why he hadn't used his magic to sail home after all these years on the island, but he conceded that it was a very good question that had recently been brought to his attention. He admitted it would have been better to have used his power for good and not revenge.

They all climbed aboard the King's ship, and Prospero used the last drop of his magic to call up a strong but gentle wind as they set sail on a swift, yet peaceful journey home to Milan.

William
Shakespeare

The famous William Shakespeare was born hundreds of years ago, in 1564. He lived in the small market town of Stratford-upon-Avon with his parents, John and Mary, and seven siblings.

Kingdome of Scotland

Dublin

Ireland

Kingdome of England

Stratford-upon-Avon

London

At only 18 years old, Shakespeare married Anne Hathaway. They had three children.

Even though the Enlightenment (one of the greatest times of learning and study) was spreading across Europe during Shakespeare's time, superstition (the belief in ghosts, spirits, and witches) was still very common in England. As a result, Shakespeare often included magical creatures in his stories to entertain the believing crowds.

During his life, Shakespeare wrote 38 plays and 154 sonnets and came up with almost 3,000 words that were added to the English language! He even invented some of the words we use today, like "bubble" and "silliness!"

Legend has it that Shakespeare's **The TeMPeSt** was inspired by a real-life shipwreck. In 1609, just a year before Shakespeare was believed to have written the play, a ship was en route to Jamestown from England when it wrecked in the Bermudas. The crew, who was believed to be lost forever, survived on a deserted island.

At the time Shakespeare was alive, it was illegal for girls to act on stage, so all of the female roles were played by boys!

The Globe Theatre is famous for being the place where many of Shakespeare's plays were performed.

To my wife, for always being there.
—L.P.

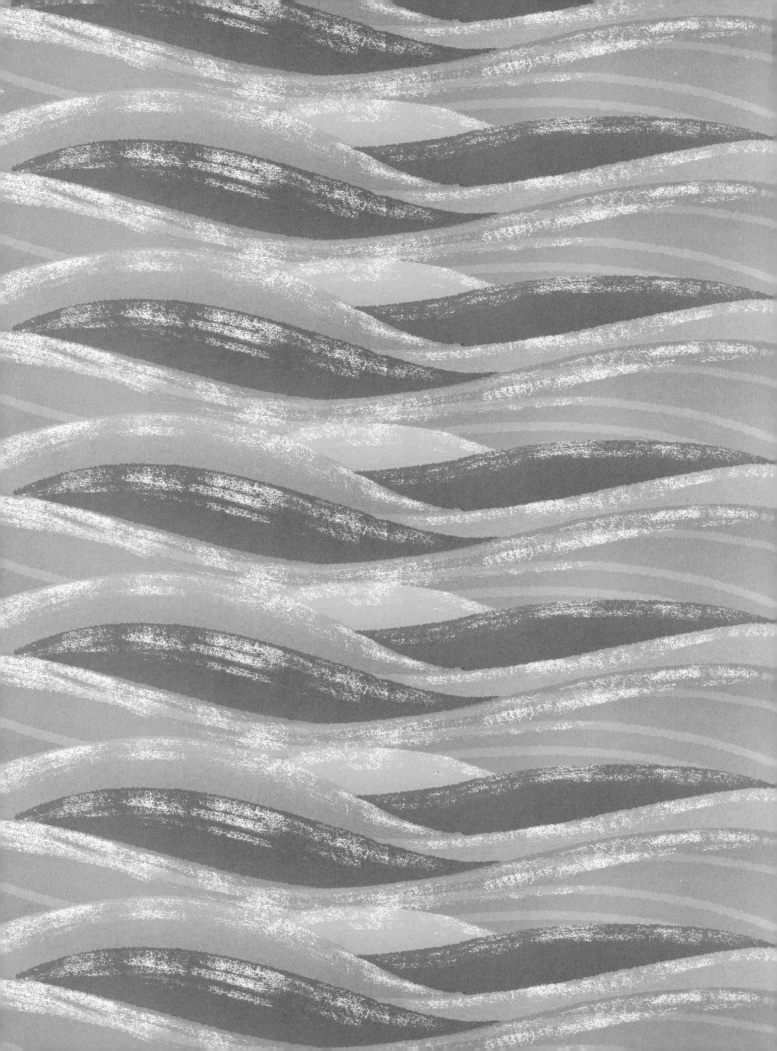